RICE

NORMAN
PRICE

BELLA
LASAGNE

JAMES

SARAH

MEET ALL THESE FRIENDS IN BUZZ BOOKS:

Thomas the Tank Engine
Tiny Toon Adventures
Looney Tunes
Bugs Bunny
Fireman Sam
Joshua Jones
Toucan 'Tecs
Flintstones
Jetsons

First published 1991 by Buzz Books,
an imprint of Reed International Books Ltd
Michelin House, 81 Fulham Road, London SW3 6RB
Reprinted 1992

LONDON MELBOURNE AUCKLAND

Fireman Sam © 1985 Prism Art & Design Ltd

Text © 1991 William Heinemann Ltd
Illustrations © 1991 William Heinemann Ltd
Based on the animation series produced by Bumper Films
for S4C/Channel 4 Wales and Prism Art & Design Ltd.
Original idea by Dave Gingell and Dave Jones,
assisted by Mike Young. Characters created by Rob Lee.
All rights reserved.

ISBN 1 85591 111 6

Printed and bound in the UK by BPCC Hazell Books Ltd

SAM'S BRASS BAND

Story by Caroline Hill-Trevor
Developed from a storyline by Rob Lee
and a script by Nia Ceidiog

Illustrations by The County Studio

"Come on, Uncle Sam, we'll challenge you to a game of cricket," said James one hot Saturday morning.

"Oh yes, good idea, it's a perfect day for cricket," Sarah agreed.

"Well, all right then," Fireman Sam
replied, "but I can't stay long – I'm meeting
the others for band practice later."

Fireman Sam went into bat, with James
bowling and Sarah looking out for a catch.

Trevor was doing some weeding in his
garden next door.

"I'm getting old, boyo," he said, standing
up and stretching. Before he knew what
was happening, a cricket ball landed in his
upturned hand. "But I haven't lost my eye
for the ball!"

"Oi, someone's out for a duck!" Trevor called over the fence. "Oh sorry, Sam," he said sheepishly. "Didn't realise it was you."

"Never mind," Fireman Sam replied. "It's your turn now, Trevor. I'm off to band practice – we're doing a special concert tomorrow."

"What's that, Norman?" asked Fireman Sam when he called at Dilys's shop.

"It's Dad's old telescope. Want a look?" Norman grinned.

"Powerful telescope this is, Norman. I can see as far as Jupiter!" joked Fireman Sam as he looked through the telescope. Norman didn't say anything.

"Hey, Norman, I said I can see Jup . . ." Fireman Sam repeated. Norman roared with laughter and ran out.

"It wasn't that funny Norman!"

"Hello Sam," said Dilys. "Ooo! How did you get a black eye?"

"Probably the same way you did, Dilys!"

"Boot polish!" exclaimed Dilys.

"Glad to see Norman hasn't lost his sense of humour," Fireman Sam laughed.

"Norman Price, come back here!" shrieked Dilys.

Back in Fireman Sam's garden, Trevor was still batting.

"Just wait, Mr Evans," thought James as he bowled the ball.

WHAM! The ball flew up onto the roof and lodged itself next to the chimney.

"OK, Mr Evans, you've won," sighed Sarah. "That's the end of the game."

"I must get your ball back first. I'll use this," shouted Trevor. He grabbed an old ladder, leaned it against the house and began to climb up.

"Uh oh! That ladder's ancient and I seem to
remember Trevor and ladders don't mix,"
said Sarah, watching from below.

"Help! I forgot, I can't stand heights!"
Trevor squeaked from the top of the ladder.

"Come down the ladder then, Mr Evans,"
called James.

"Not until I've got your ball," said Trevor bravely.

He scrambled onto the roof and reached out for the ball. Before he could grab it, the ball rolled off the roof, down the drainpipe and straight into James's hands.

"Out Trevor, at last!" cheered James.

"Just you wait!" Trevor said crossly. "I'm coming down."

But as he spun round, he slipped down the roof and kicked the ladder over. It fell to the ground and smashed to pieces.

"Now what shall we do?" gasped James.

"Well, don't just stand there, do something!" shouted Trevor, clinging to the guttering with his eyes closed. "I can't hang on much longer."

"I'll call the fire brigade," Sarah shouted. She ran inside Fireman Sam's house.

Up at the fire station, the Pontypandy Brass Band were practising for the concert.

"We're not very good are we?" grumbled Station Officer Steele, putting cotton wool in his ears.

"Practice makes perfect, Sir," said Penny.

"Once more then," Station Officer Steele sighed, picking up his baton.

"Firefighter Cridlington, try to keep up with us," he bellowed above the noise.

Elvis smiled at Penny and fully extended the slide on his trombone. There was a loud crash and the band stopped playing.

Elvis had punctured Penny's drum!

"Tha . . . that's torn it, Sir," stuttered Elvis, blushing bright red.

"Drum's patched up, Sir. Ready when you are," said Penny Morris a few minutes later.

"Very well. After two – one, two."

But instead of the brass band, the fire alarm sounded.

"Action stations," Station Officer Steele cried.

"Fireman trapped on roof," read Penny. "It must be Trevor!"

"Firefighter Morris, deal with any other calls; everyone else, into Jupiter," ordered Station Officer Steele.

"Knowing Trevor's head for heights, we haven't got long," said Fireman Sam.

20

"Aargh! I'm falling!" Trevor yelled.

"Prepare ladders. Extend!" commanded
Station Officer Steele.

Moving quickly, the fire brigade put the
ladder against Fireman Sam's house.
"Thank goodness you're here, Uncle Sam,"
cried Sarah when they arrived. "Trevor's
sliding off your roof!"

"Oh no, not the ladder," Trevor pleaded.

"Are you an Auxiliary Firefighter or not, Evans?" snorted Station Officer Steele.

"Anything but the ladder," Trevor shuddered, looking over the edge.

"Come on, Trevor, you've done it before, remember?" Fireman Sam said kindly.

"That's what I'm worried about!"

"Don't look down, boyo," Trevor muttered to himself. "Just don't look down!"

Fireman Sam and Elvis looked at each other. "Hey, Trevor, it's Bella's special spaghetti bolognaise for supper tonight," Elvis called out.

Suddenly, Trevor slipped off the roof but managed to cling on to the ladder.

"I'm losing my appetite!" he moaned as he slid quickly down the ladder. "Ooooh," he wailed, landing with a bump in the middle of the firefighters.

"Still haven't got the hang of it, have we, Evans?" Station Officer Steele remarked.

"Well, that's that problem solved, Sir!" said Fireman Sam.

"But what about the concert tomorrow?" said Station Officer Steele, looking worried. "I know practice makes perfect, but we haven't got much time."

"If I could have the afternoon in my inventing shed, I think we could be in with a chance."

Fireman Sam whispered his idea to Station Officer Steele as the rest of them lowered the ladder.

The next day at the concert in the park, the Pontypandy Brass Band were playing beautifully.

"Not bad, are they?" said Dilys.

"Too modest, they are," said Trevor.

As he played, someone behind the bandstand caught Fireman Sam's eye.

Norman had discovered his latest invention! Fireman Sam signalled for him not to give the game away.

Norman grinned. "I wish you could invent a machine to do my homework, Fireman Sam!" he whispered, and joined in the applause.

FIREMAN SAM

STATION OFFICER STEELE

TREVOR EVANS

ELVIS CRIDLINGTON

PENNY MORRIS